The Legend of the Jersey Devil

Written by Trinka Hakes Noble and Illustrated by Gerald Kelley

For Jerry—with love,

T.H.N.

☾

For Richard—For all the patience and help
with this book, in life, and everything.

G.K.

Sleeping Bear Press®
315 E. Eisenhower Parkway, Suite 200
Ann Arbor, MI 48108
www.sleepingbearpress.com

Printed and bound in the United States.

10 9 8 7 6 5 4 3 2 1

Library of Congress Cataloging-in-Publication Data

Noble, Trinka Hakes.
The legend of the Jersey Devil / written by Trinka Hakes Noble ;
illustrated by Gerald Kelley.
pages cm
Summary: Relates the origins of the Jersey Devil, a monstrous creature that
has reportedly haunted the Pine Barrens region of New Jersey since 1735 menacing
townspeople, worrying livestock, and causing all manner of ills.
ISBN 978-1-58536-837-2
[1. Jersey Devil (Monster)—Fiction. 2. Monsters—Fiction.
3. Pine Barrens (N.J.)—Fiction.] I. Kelley, Gerald, illustrator. II. Title.
PZ7.N6715Ler 2013
[Fic]--dc23   2013004093

There is a wild and mysterious place in New Jersey that has kept its ancient ways. Long spiny fingers of briny ocean mist creep through its dark pine groves on currents as old as time. Water that flowed on earth eons ago still slithers through its tangled roots like poisonous snakes.

And, lurking in its black swamps and murky bogs are hidden secrets and evil stories that can only be told on the darkest of nights …

… for 'tis believed the place is haunted.

Some believe the ghosts of pirates, smugglers, and scoundrels roam the backwoods, lonely roads, and inland waterways on moonless nights. Unearthly sounds, like the shrieks and wails of witches, have been heard above the howling winds.

Others say the spirits of Lenape medicine men appear in the swampy mist where long ago they cast spells, sending foul vapors over the villages of their enemies. Many believe the early settlers cursed the place by calling it the Pine Barrens, because no good, wholesome crops could be grown in its poor sandy soil.

So the few early colonists and their descendants who settled in the Pine Barrens were a hardy lot. On dark nights these brave folks gathered around their evening fires and passed down many ghoulish tales, haunting legends, and scary stories.

But the most frightening story of all has been told in the Pine Barrens for nearly 300 years. It's not about any ordinary witch, ghost, or goblin. Oh no! This terrifying tale is about the supreme specter of all …

the very devil himself …

…the Jersey Devil!

Long ago, in 1735, when the British Crown ruled New Jersey, a strange and terrifying event took place on a remote stretch of land called Leeds Point.

In a poor hamlet of woodsmen's cottages and fishermen's huts there lived a woman who had twelve children. Folks called her Mother Leeds. One dark autumn night, close to All Hallows' Eve, or Halloween, a fierce storm blew in from the Atlantic. Its savage winds and pounding rains tore at every shingle and shutter in this poor little settlement.

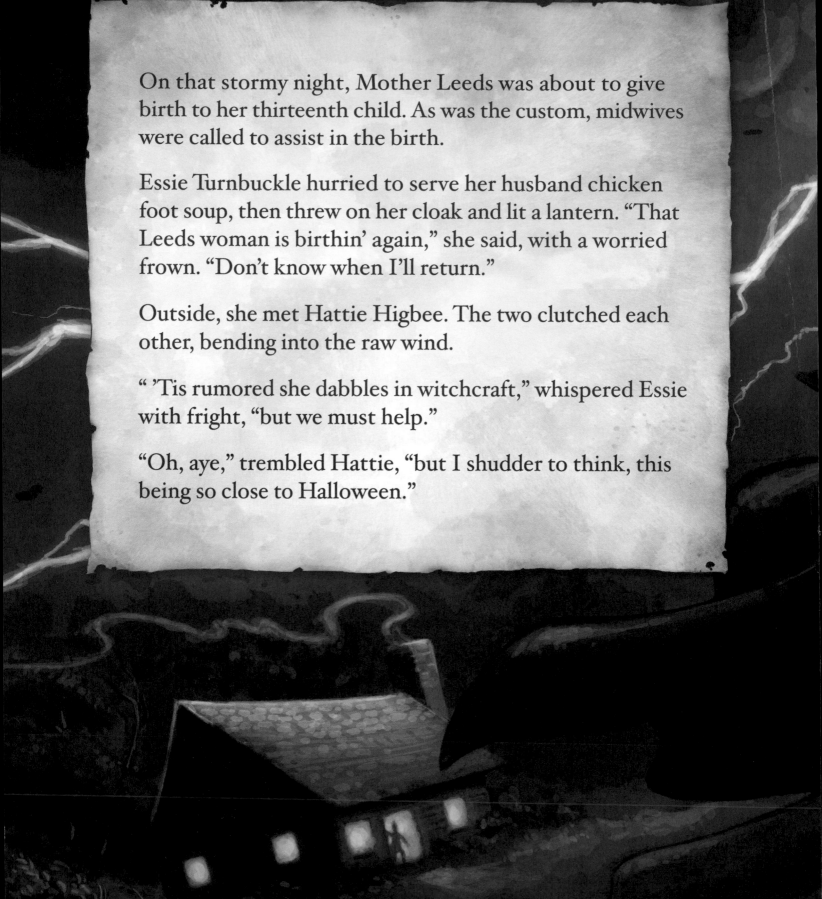

On that stormy night, Mother Leeds was about to give birth to her thirteenth child. As was the custom, midwives were called to assist in the birth.

Essie Turnbuckle hurried to serve her husband chicken foot soup, then threw on her cloak and lit a lantern. "That Leeds woman is birthin' again," she said, with a worried frown. "Don't know when I'll return."

Outside, she met Hattie Higbee. The two clutched each other, bending into the raw wind.

" 'Tis rumored she dabbles in witchcraft," whispered Essie with fright, "but we must help."

"Oh, aye," trembled Hattie, "but I shudder to think, this being so close to Halloween."

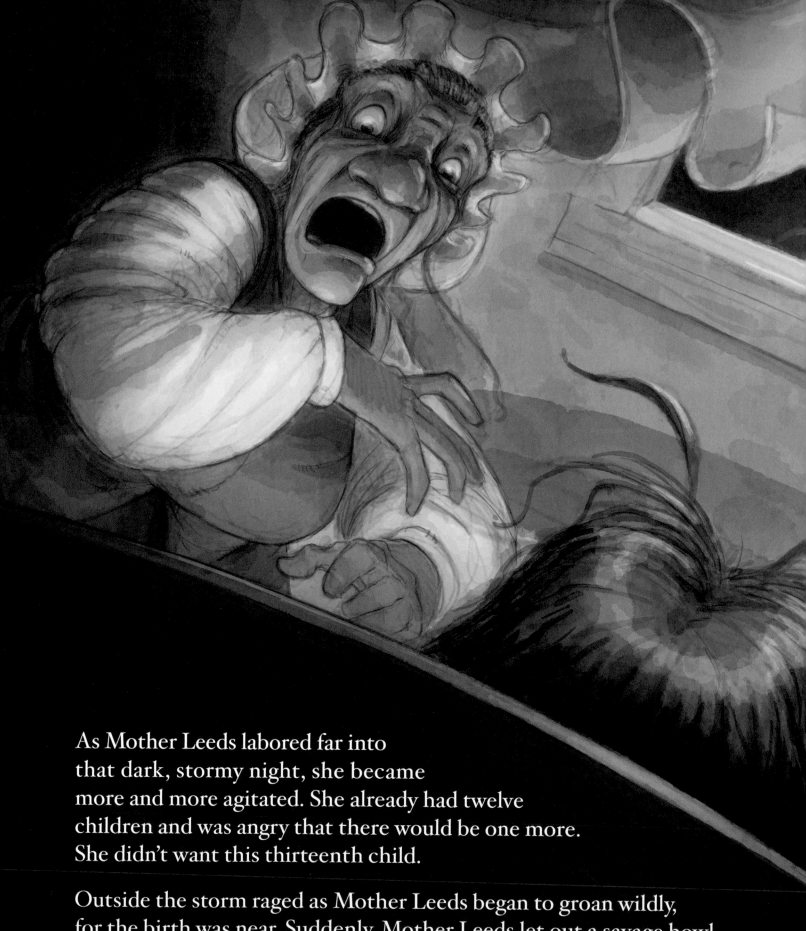

As Mother Leeds labored far into
that dark, stormy night, she became
more and more agitated. She already had twelve
children and was angry that there would be one more.
She didn't want this thirteenth child.

Outside the storm raged as Mother Leeds began to groan wildly,
for the birth was near. Suddenly, Mother Leeds let out a savage howl
and screamed, "Oh, let it be a devil!"

In a flash of lightning and clap of thunder,
Mother Leeds's thirteenth child was born...
but it was no ordinary child!

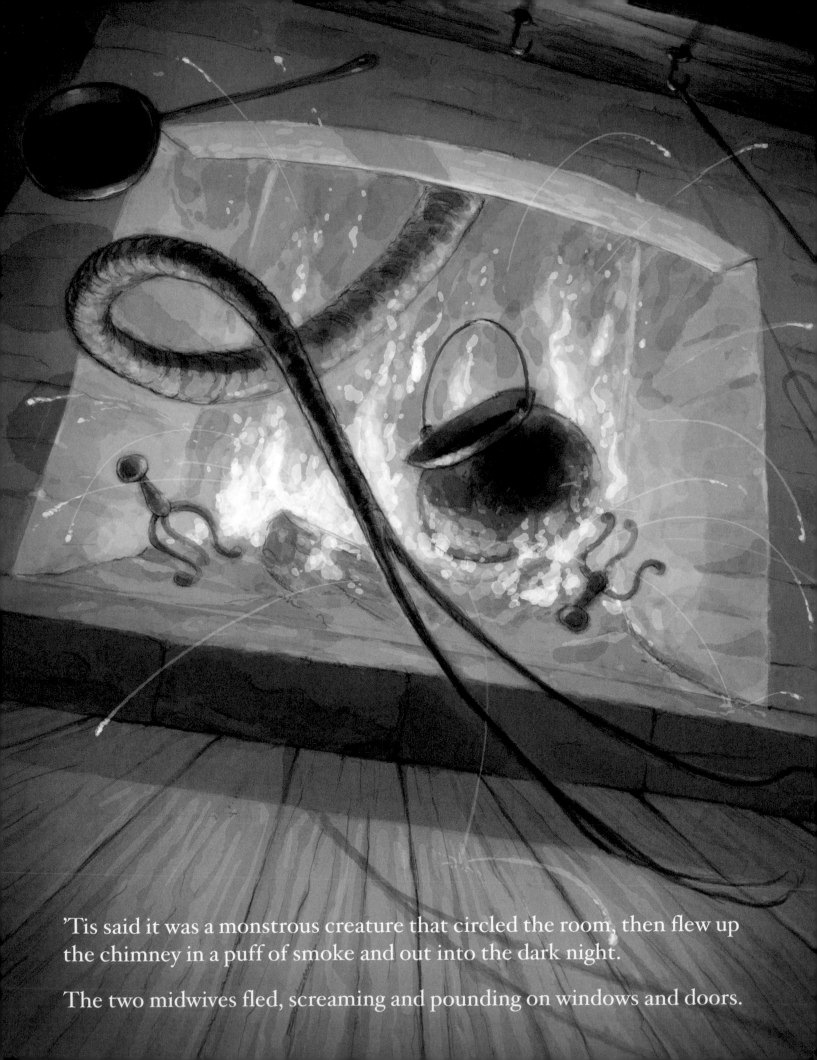

'Tis said it was a monstrous creature that circled the room, then flew up the chimney in a puff of smoke and out into the dark night.

The two midwives fled, screaming and pounding on windows and doors.

"Awake ye all!" they shrieked. "The Devil's among us! The Devil's among us!"

Candles flickered wildly and lanterns swung violently, casting eerie shadows as folks rushed to heed the alarm.

"What's all this?" demanded the mayor.

"Oh … oh … such a hideous creature!" stammered Essie, trembling from head to toe. "It had the bony head of a horse … a … a long scaly body and big bat wings sproutin' out his back!"

"Nay! Nay! More hideous than that!" gasped Hattie, shaking like a leaf. "It had a forked tail, claws for hands, and the hooves of a goat!"

"I know hideous when I see it," bickered Essie. "It had two horns growing out of his head and eyes that burned red!"

"Nay! They glowed yellow!" disagreed Hattie.

"Red, I say!" insisted Essie.

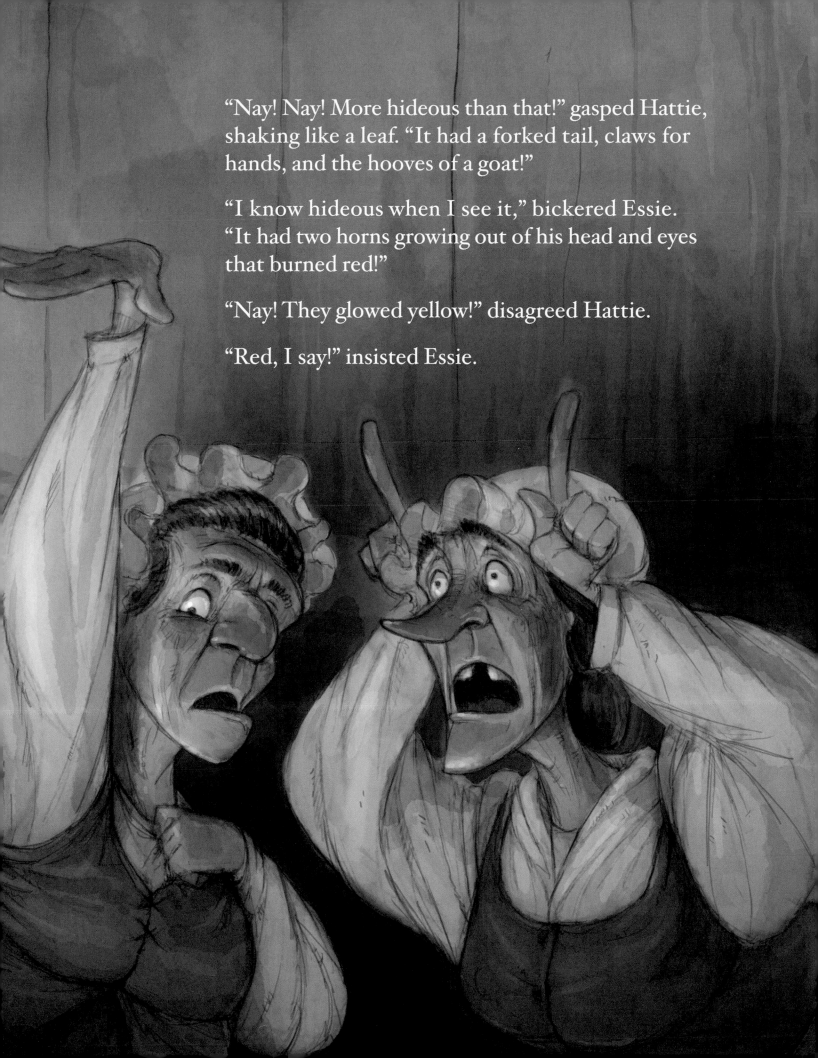

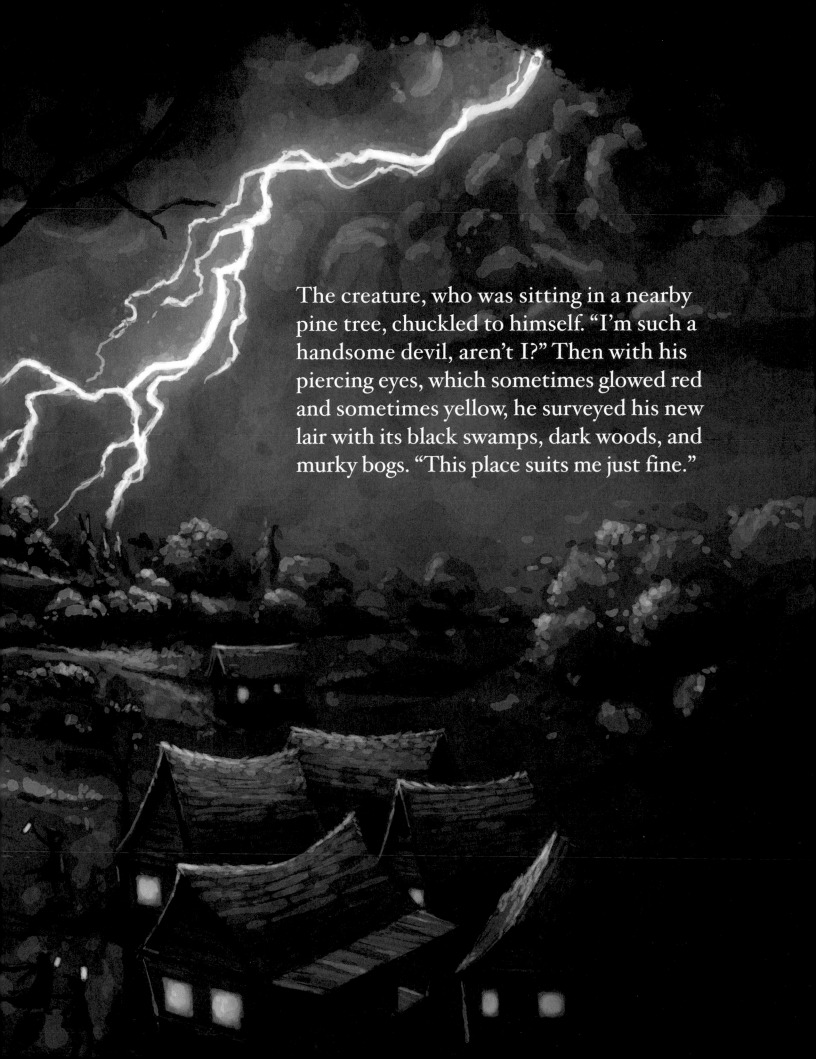

The creature, who was sitting in a nearby pine tree, chuckled to himself. "I'm such a handsome devil, aren't I?" Then with his piercing eyes, which sometimes glowed red and sometimes yellow, he surveyed his new lair with its black swamps, dark woods, and murky bogs. "This place suits me just fine."

In the weeks and months that followed, strange things began to happen.

If crops failed, folks said it was the devil's fault. If chickens stopped laying eggs, the devil was to blame. He scared the sheep, caused wells to go dry, spooked horses, and turned over carts. He soured milk, stole pies, and toppled clotheslines. Children were kept indoors.

As more stories were told and more sightings witnessed, news of the Jersey Devil spread quickly across the Pine Barrens. All mysterious events were blamed on him. Posses were sent out, but they always came back empty-handed.

When a traveling preacher, plodding along on his old nag, got wind of the news, he proclaimed, "I can rid you good folks of this evil demon!"

He held a huge prayer meeting. Folks came from far and wide. He preached a fiery sermon that went on and on and on from morn 'til night, until finally he passed around his black preacher's hat. Folks gladly dropped in coins, relieved he'd finally finished!

For a time all was quiet.

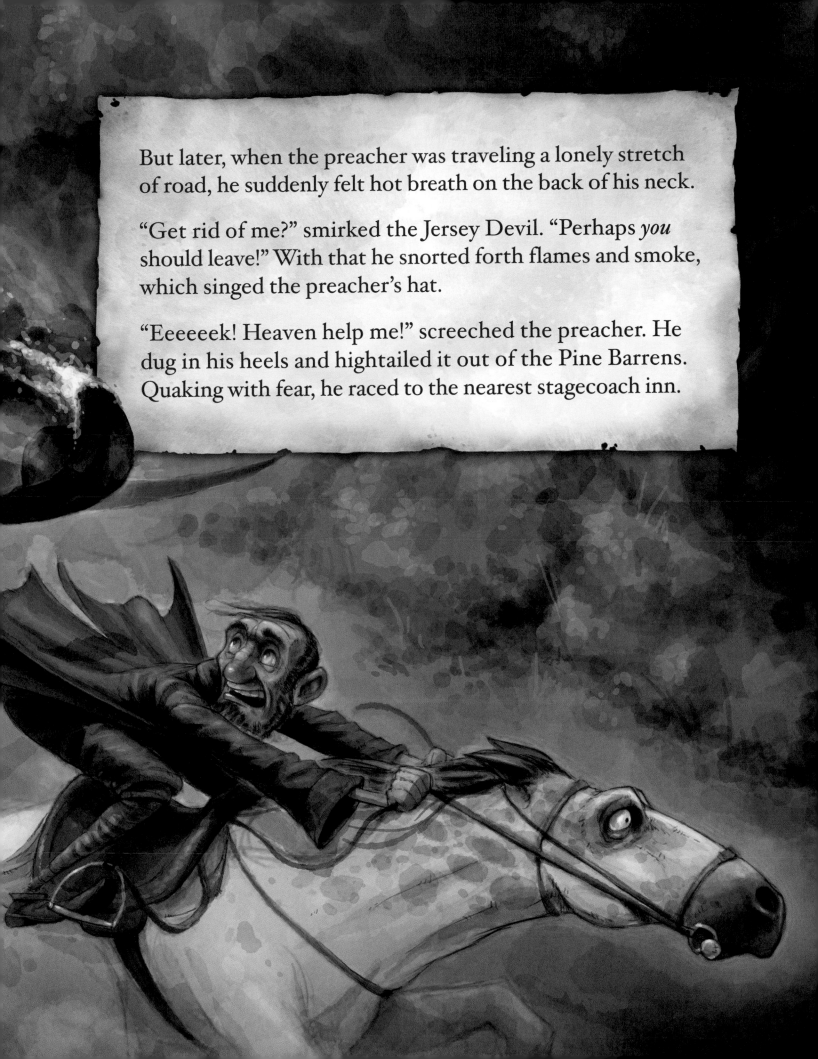

But later, when the preacher was traveling a lonely stretch of road, he suddenly felt hot breath on the back of his neck.

"Get rid of me?" smirked the Jersey Devil. "Perhaps *you* should leave!" With that he snorted forth flames and smoke, which singed the preacher's hat.

"Eeeeeek! Heaven help me!" screeched the preacher. He dug in his heels and hightailed it out of the Pine Barrens. Quaking with fear, he raced to the nearest stagecoach inn.

The innkeeper thrust a tankard of local applejack into the preacher's quivering hands.

"Here, preacher, have a sip of Jersey Lightning. It'll steady your nerves."

The preacher stood in front of the fire and told of his harrowing encounter with the Jersey Devil to all the inn's guests.

Listening intently were a couple of city slickers. One was a circus owner from Philadelphia and the other a land speculator from New York. Both were sly wheeler-dealers. Immediately, each started hatching a plan to capture the Jersey Devil.

The Jersey Devil will be my star attraction! plotted the Philadelphia circus owner. *I'll charge a high fee and have money to burn!*

He jumped to his feet and shouted, "A reward of one hundred gold crowns to anyone who captures the Jersey Devil, preferably alive!"

Not to be outdone by Philadelphia, the New York wheeler-dealer leaped to his feet.

"I'll double it to two hundred gold crowns, dead or alive!" he shouted, for he had plans to stuff the devil, exhibit him in New York, and charge a high fee. *I'll be rich, the toast of the town!* he schemed.

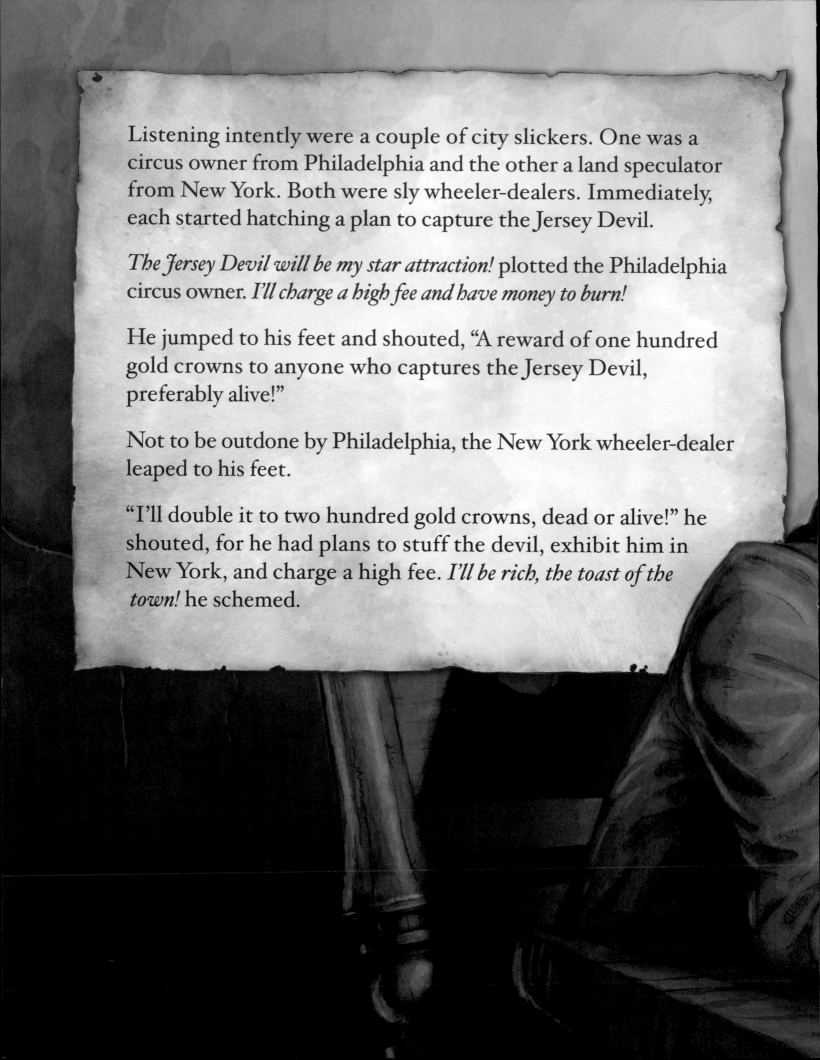

In no time, devil hunters from New York descended on the Pine Barrens in droves. Fortune seekers from Philadelphia came with cages, chains, and traps. They trampled crops and knocked over fences. They cut down trees and drained swamps. They spooked horses, tipped over carts, and mistakenly captured cows, chickens, and sheep. Children were kept indoors. Why, they even stole a few pies for their supper…until the good folks of the Pine Barrens had had enough of these outsiders.

"Better the devil we know than the devil we don't," they agreed and decided to accept the Jersey Devil as one of their own.

The Jersey Devil was touched when he heard this, so he did the good folks of the Pine Barrens a favor. In a fiery rage, he chased those outsiders back to Philadelphia and New York.

And, to make sure they never returned, he made many terrifying appearances down through the years. The most famous was during the third week of January, back in 1909.

What should have been a peaceful winter's week was anything but.

That week the Jersey Devil was sighted outside the Pine Barrens in thirty or more towns. Thousands of people reported seeing either the Jersey Devil himself or his numerous strange tracks in the snow. He hovered and hissed above a trolley car. He perched on backyard sheds and clotheslines, sending housewives into swoons. Factories and schools were closed. Newspapers ran front-page articles. Police were on high alert. Posses were sent out but dogs refused to track the creature.

Even though descriptions and accountings differed, all agreed it was the Jersey Devil.

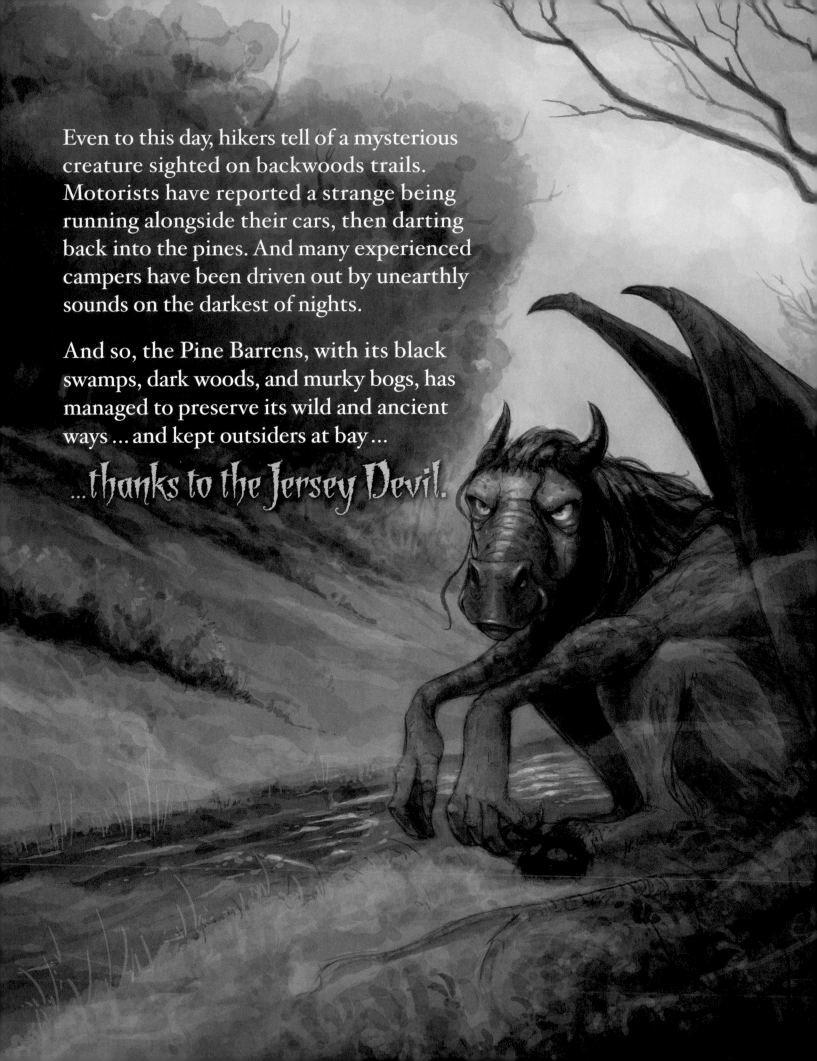

Even to this day, hikers tell of a mysterious creature sighted on backwoods trails. Motorists have reported a strange being running alongside their cars, then darting back into the pines. And many experienced campers have been driven out by unearthly sounds on the darkest of nights.

And so, the Pine Barrens, with its black swamps, dark woods, and murky bogs, has managed to preserve its wild and ancient ways ... and kept outsiders at bay ...

...thanks to the Jersey Devil.